# LITTLE SWINE

A Southern Gothic

ULTAN BANAN

# LITTLE SWINE

Little Swine scrubbed the floor. The boy watched.

Little Swine was a good little swine and did what was told.

The room reeked of sweat and old food. Toilet stench and damp walls. A small window, high up and blacked out. Permanently shut. A low cot on the floor, a tattered pillow and filthy sheets. A lamp in the corner with a faded child's shade. Butterflies. A doll on a chair.

The sound of his breathing. And now the scratch of the scrubbing brush on the floor. He watches.

Little Piggie gets right in the corners, he said.

Little Swine pushed into the corners with the scrubbing brush, the sound of the wet bristles harsh against the concrete. A taciturn lather in its wake.

Little Swine wore her nightie. Little Swine always wore her nightie. He liked to watch her in her nightie. He scratched himself as he watched. Heavy breathing.

She worked her way along the wall toward the chair. She was plump and wobbled as she moved.

Piggie moves the chair and scrubs underneath, he said.

Little Swine did.

Boy went to the bed and sat down. Always watching. She did not turn to look at him. He lifted her stained pillow and pushed his face into it and inhaled. He grunted. Touched himself. His left foot clawed at the floor like a goat. Little Swine, eyes down, worked. He sniffed the pillow again. She trembled. Upstairs above, Momma-who-was-not-Momma dragged chairs over the kitchen floor. She was cleaning too. Once a month it was like this.

When Little Swine was done in the corner, she replaced the chair. She worked her way along the other wall toward the toilet. Boy watched. Then he pushed his nose in his armpit and smelled himself.

From upstairs too the sound of an old transistor. Weather. Maybe sports. A jingle. Momma-who-was-not-Momma whistled. She dropped something and swore. Boy looked toward the ceiling. Little Swine froze, only for a second. Then she went back to the scrubbing.

Little Piggie gets right in the toilet, Boy said.

Little Swine reached in the toilet and gave it a good scrub out. He watched her nightie ride up the back of her heavy thighs. Little Swine gagged and Boy grunted. When it was done, she pulled the flush. She turned, eyes to the floor. She advanced into the middle of the room. The scratching of the brush on the concrete floor. The water in the bucket now black. No more suds.

Boy sat cradling Swine's pillow. Swine on her hands and knees, her knees scuffed raw. Her hands red with bleach. The stink of bleach. Little Swine was a good little swine.

Little Piggie licks the floor, Boy said.

Little Swine did. Boy parted his legs as she approached, the pillow on his lap. Swine looked up but not into his eyes. Boy reached out and took her by the hair and rested her head on the pillow. He stroked her dank, unwashed hair.

Good little piggie, he whispered.

She fought her trembling. Boy put his fingers in her mouth. She clung to his calves.

Good piggie, he said again.

He pushed her away and stood up, dropping the pillow on the bed.

Little Piggie bends over the bed, he said.

She heard him and did. Good Little Swine always did. Boy stood over her, his hand under his shirt. She scrunched up her eyes, pushed her face into the mattress.

Piggie lifts her nightie, Boy said.

Little Swine reached behind her.

Boy!

The shout from above. Boy looked to the door. Little Swine froze.

Boy!

Momma?

Get up here…

Momma-who-was-not-Momma didn't like to ask twice. Boy looked at Little Swine. Boy looked at the door. Boy looked at Little Swine then turned to the door. He went out and closed it.

The sound of the bolt sliding in the latch.

Little Swine still with her face in the mattress.

That little bitch do her cleaning? Momma-who-was-not-Momma said.

Boy grunted. Boy went to the bread bin and took out a loaf. He sat at the table, pulled out three slices of bread in his fat fist and began to eat. Momma-who-was-not-Momma glared at him, snatched the loaf from him and put it back in the breadbin.

Lunch in an hour, she said. Come here and help me move this sideboard.

Boy pushed the rest of the bread in his mouth, got up and lifted one end of the sideboard and they dragged it to the wall. The plastic coverlet knotted and curled up where the edge met the wall. Momma took the flowers from the counter and placed them back on the sideboard. On the wall above the sideboard a picture: Momma and an unknown man. Boy sat down again.

Don't you be sittin down, boy. You know what needs doin.

Boy got up, pulled up his pants. He went to the door and opened it, and disappeared outside. Momma took the picture from the wall and gave the frame a rub with a cloth, then put it back on the wall. She went to the fridge. On the fridge, an urn. She dusted it and replaced it.

From outside, the sound of splitting wood.

Momma grunted. An indistinct muttering issued from her: *Boy… good thing… critter… fuckstick.*

In front of a grimy mirror next to a row of cupboards, Momma took out some lipstick and applied it sloppily. She took down the picture again and kissed it, the glass crusted with years of devotion. Momma put it back then went to the fridge, took out the meat. Slapped it down on a chopping board. Fingered it. Seasoned it. Put it in a dish, lashed it with cooking oil and opened the oven. The heat scorched her face. She shoved the dish in and turned to press the door closed with her ass. She paused there, her ass on the oven door. She sighed. Then she lit a cigarette.

Momma. Smoker's lips. Dogyard hair. A tit-job gone wrong. Momma's eyes and the fire in them. Momma looking out the back window at Boy. Momma's hatred of Boy and Momma-who-was-not-Momma's twisted devotion to him. Boy, out back chopping wood, fat and oblivious. Boy who would never be right. Momma who would never accept him but who couldn't yet let him go.

Downstairs, a noise.

Momma listens, cigarette grazing her lips.

Momma took a long puff of the cigarette, her arms clasped about her body.

Jesus fucking Christ, she whispered, watching Boy nearly cleave off his right foot.

Momma didn't ask for no children, but all her life Momma was lumbered with fucksticks and rejects and wasn't she the bitterer for it.

Momma the woman of steel resolve.

Momma stubbed out the cigarette, the butt flush with her rank lipstick.

Boy, get the fuck in here before you do yourself an injury, she shouted.

The chopping ceased. Momma went to the fridge and poured a glass of milk and put it on the table. Boy came in.

Sit the fuck down and drink your milk.

Bread, Boy said.

You're gonna eat in a bit, you fucking imbecile. Sit down and drink your milk.

Boy sat down and drank his milk.


After eating, Momma took the scraps and put them back in the dish, threw in a couple slices of bread, covered in it cooking oil.

Here, take this out back.

Boy sucked through his teeth, got up and took the tray. He went out the back door.

Goddamn mouths to feed, Momma muttered.

She stacked up the plates and put them in the sink. Flies buzzed up, settling again. On the counter next to the breadbin, Weasel in his cage squeaked. Momma glared at him and Weasel ceased.

Momma lit a cigarette and scratched her armpit, the cigarette inches from her flesh. She coughed and spat in the sink.

Momma, all alone in the world. Her wards, her burdens. Momma the caregiver. Momma, suckler of lost souls. By her they lived, and for her they gave. Momma would never be free.

From the shed outside, a clatter. Momma went to look out the open window. Boy emerged from the shed and let the door swing shut. From inside, only the sound of scratching and scraping, and a bestial grunting.

Boy came in and stood in the door, looking at Momma-who-was-not-Momma.

Momma glared back.

Momma wanna rub? Boy said.

Momma spat out an angry puff of smoke.

Momma wants a rub, she said.

Don't put your feet near me, Momma-who-was-not-Momma said, putting out a cigarette. You know I hate feet.

Yes Momma.

I need to go and wash.

Momma got up and fixed herself, and hurried away from the couch. She whispered some foul lament as she went out. Boy sat up and looked around him stupidly. Boy with no mind of his own. Boy, an automaton, driven by some combination of a desire to keep Momma happy and the satisfaction of his base needs and desires.

He scratched himself, filled suddenly by the absence of Momma-who-was-not-Momma. Boy looked down at the couch where she'd just lain. He touched the foul upholstery, his chest buoyant, his breath labored. Boy lived with loss. The loss of the thing that was not there, had never been there and would never be. Boy's life was a hole that would never be filled. It hurt Boy none at all.

From downstairs, a sound. Boy's ears pricked up. Boy liked to be with Little Swine but time with her was at Momma's say-so. The tick-tock of Momma's clock was dictated by neither timepiece nor planet, nor man nor boy. Momma said and Boy played. He slid his hand under his shirt and rested it on his belly. A sign of unfulfilled needs.

Boy listened to the water come on in the room next door. Momma in the shower. Boy fidgeted, the urge on him to sneak to the door and watch. He began to rock, and covered his ear that he might not hear the sound. He could escape the sounds but couldn't escape the pictures. He began to hum. It did no good. Momma-who-was-not-Momma before him in all her nakedness. Boy stood up, turned this way, turned that way. *Momma's fleshy pillows. His head between Momma's pillows. Momma's feet that could never be touched. Momma's hands on him. Momma's hands in him…*

Nggghh…

Boy uttered a pained whimper and stormed into the kitchen and out the back door. He passed the shed and went straight to the chicken coop, opened it and pulled out a big hen. Holding her by the legs, he smashed her off the frame of the coop until blood flew. Then he beat her some more. When he was spattered head to toe in her blood, he dropped the body and began to whine. He slid to his ass on the ground. There he would remain til Momma found him. Then she would go to work on him.

Don't you dare fucking move.

Momma left the room. Boy lay there, strapped to the bed and run through with needles head to foot. Needles through the flesh around his armpits. Needles through the hide of his ears and in the soles of his feet, and through his genitals and the skin between his fingers. Forced right into his fleshy buttocks. One through his lip. Boy bit the pillow, the pillow wet with his tears. He groaned:

*Nggggggghhh...*

and scraped his torso over the tattered mattress.

Maybe Boy was hot for it. Of pain and pleasure he knew not the difference. Still he cried. A dull agony was Boy's lot, whether in pain or pleasure, it was there underneath it all, the reason of his being.

Boy. Dumb fuck. Imbecile. Redundant prick. Sorry sack of shit.

Boy was happy in some dumb fucking way. In some chattel way. A slug's content.

His fleshy body dotted with blood. Swollen welts rising around the pin pricks.

Mom returned and emptied a bottle of vinegar over him and he squealed, in delight or anguish even God knew not.

When she'd finished pulling the pins from his horrid

anatomy she untied him hand and foot.

Put your pants on and go and take that little bitch for a walk before feedin, Momma said. And don't you even think about gon' pokin around with her, you hear me? I'll tell you when it's time.

Boy, wordless, got up. He put on his pants and his vest and went below.

The heavy clunk of the bolt.

When he went in Little Swine was on the bed clutching the teddy, chest heaving, as if she'd just raced there. Boy went and stood in front of her. Little Swine put Teddy down and fell to the floor on her knees. Boy gripped a clump of her thick greasy red hair and proceeded to drag her across the room. She followed obediently, crawling around after him. Boy grunted, turned to look at her rump shake in her tattered nightie.

Piggie walks across the floor like a good little piggie, Boy said.

He tugged her hair and she whimpered.

Little Swine is a good little piggie because Momma feeds her and keeps her safe, Boy said. And because Boy looks after her and takes her walkies and sneaks her biscuits.

They walked in a square around the walls of her cell. Sometimes Boy would change direction and cut a diagonal across the room, pulling her with him. The scabs on her knees opened up and began to bleed. Her scuffed hands clawed the cold concrete of the floor, tracing a track around and across the room like a blind cat. Little Swine was not blind, she simply cared not to see. She kept her eyes to the floor.

From above, the smell of food. Momma had made dinner. Momma-who-was-not-Momma would feed her children.

Boy stopped at the bed, raised his head to the ceiling. He felt a stinging in his ankle and looked down. Little Swine at his feet, eyes to the floor. Good little piggie. Fat rump under her nightie. *Little Swine bends over on the bed and pulls down her unmentionables. Boy climbs up on Little Swine…*

They heard Momma come down the stairs. Steps in the corridor. Then Momma was in the door, in her hand a plate of food. Boy looked at her. Boy went out to the corridor and dragged in Little Swine's trough. Momma handed him the pot.

Straight upstairs when you're done, you hear?

Yes Momma.

Momma left and Boy tipped the contents of the pot into the trough. He returned to the bed and took Little Swine by the hair and led her to the trough.

Little Piggie eats her dinner, Boy said.

Little Swine did. Stuck her head in the trough and ate. Boy watched.

Boy grunted and scratched his belly.

Late at night, when Boy was locked in his room and Momma was alone, Momma liked to paint her toenails. Boy wasn't allowed to touch Momma's feet. Momma-who-was-not-Momma wouldn't have it. Momma put out the cigarette and drew up her feet, and laid out her varnishes on the bed before her. Tonight she fancied purple. Often when she'd done violence to the boy she chose purple. The color chosen, she set about cleaning off the old paint, and when she'd cleaned each toe down and dried them off she lay back against the pillows and lit another cigarette. She stared at the ceiling as she puffed, her puckered lips sucking the life out of the cancerstick, and each one sucking the life out of her. Every smoker is a slow suicide, and Momma craved death no less than anyone else but Momma believed death would never come. How long this life, and in each cigarette Momma seemed to discern there was no seeming end to this mortal coil, and that it would go on turning with its endless parade of vexations and provocations, filled with fuckwits and little swine and useless fucking children, turning all while she stood by and suffered the inescapable horror of its dull monotony. Then the cigarette would come to an end and she would stab it out with venom, perceiving perhaps that each stick was a reminder of her death that was far too far away and would not come quick enough, and that no matter how she might will it this life would just not let her go. Momma never hated the world so much as the moment she stabbed out a cigarette.

The cigarette out, Momma blew a vicious puff of smoke at the ceiling and lifted the purple polish.

Momma didn't sleep and Momma didn't dream. Momma rested. Often she would wake and hear Boy snoring, and when she did she would think about hurting Boy. Those hurts were explored and played out and stored away for later times. Momma's arsenal was vast and devastating. Momma knew how to bring hurt.

Meanwhile, Boy dreamed. Boy dreamed a slug's dreams and woke up from his sluggish rest, his chest heaving and his breath labored, and he listened carefully for any sound from Momma's room. Boy didn't move until Momma was up. When he heard her in the kitchen making coffee, only then would his head rise off the pillow.

He sat up and put his feet in his slippers and scratched himself. He lifted his plastic child's glasses from the cabinet and put them on his face. When he'd made toilet, he went to the kitchen. Momma had food ready.

Here, take this to the Beast.

Momma held out a plate. Boy took it.

Yes Momma.

Boy went out to the shed with the plate. When he came back, Momma had his breakfast on the table. Boy sat down and ate.

Momma leaned against the counter and smoked, occasionally glancing at the fat rolls on the back of his neck with disgust.

When you've finished, wood needs takin in, Momma said.

Boy grunted.

From the shed beyond, a clatter and a screech.

You teasin him with his food? I hope to fuck you ain't teasin him with his food.

No Momma, Boy said, spitting his breakfast.

If I go out and see you been teasin him, I swear to fuck…

Boy gobbled his breakfast.

Momma stood by the counter puffing, her leg trembling anxiously. She put out the cigarette.

Right. If you're done I want you to go over to the shed. Damned kid was wailing all night long. Thing ain't gonna live. Go over there and take care of it.

Boy pushed his plate away and stood, and moved toward Momma in some kind of fallow embrace. She slapped him.

Fuck do you think you're doin? Go on get outta here.

Momma turned to the counter to look at Weasel. Boy slunk from the kitchen, head low.

Boy entered the animal shed hearing the sound of bleating from the kid. Only days old, the thing was ill in health and poorly. The third of a litter of three, it wouldn't make it. Boy would end it swiftly. Momma did make a good kid stew.

He peered over the stall to see the three young animals. His tongue came out the side of his mouth in a grotesque and twisted manner. He looked around him, before going to the bench and picking up a claw hammer. Taking it to the stall, he opened the gate and stepped inside.

He sat down on the floor. Two of the goats approached him and climbed over him. The sick one lay in the corner.

Momma said she gon' do somethin nice for my birthday, yes she did, Boy said.

The goats hopped about him. Boy pulled one into his lap and pushed his finger into the goat's mouth.

Momma gon' take care of Boy, yes she is. Boy gon' be a man soon, Momma said so.

The ailing sound from the corner continued. Boy looked at the animal.

Momma puts the baby goat in the pot and cooks her up nice, Boy said, standing up and lifting the hammer. He advanced toward the goat.

Did you hear what I said, little goatie?

He leaned down to the sickly kid.

Momma puts the goat in the pie and bakes her up good…

Mouth open, Boy heavy-breathed, his hands on his knees.

Oh yes she does. Momma bakes her up nice and Boy eats, and when he's done, he… when he's done, Momma…

Boy took the kid by the hind legs and dragged it into the center of the stall. He put his foot on its neck and brought the hammer down hard, shattering the animal's skull. The other two kids screeched and fled into the corner. Next stall over, Boy heard the billy goat holler.

Boy dragged the kid out of the stall to the middle of the shed. He put the hammer on the table and picked up the skinning knife.

The kids trembled in their stall. The billy goat bleated.

When the skinning and gutting was done, Boy got to boning and hung the meat. He wiped his hand on a dirty rag.

Momma holds Boy and kisses him and tells him he's a good boy, Boy said, wiping the knife. And then she lays him down and gives him the weasel, he muttered.

He put down the knife and went over the stall where the billy goat stood tethered. Boy looked in and blew a kiss at billy goat. His bloody hand slid under his vest and stroked his belly.

Momma opened the door of Little Swine's cell and looked in. Little Swine was sitting on the edge of the bed holding Teddy. She turned her head to the door but didn't look at Momma. Momma stood in the doorway and stared. Then she stepped inside.

Little Swine held Teddy tighter.

Momma stopped in front of Little Swine then knelt down.

You know what to do, go on now, Momma said.

Hesitantly, Little Swine put down Teddy and opened her legs.

And the rest, Momma said.

Little Swine pushed her underwear down around her ankles and parted her thighs.

Wider, Momma said, her voice stinging. Fuckin thighs on you. Size you're gettin to, I swear to Christ we're too damned good to you.

Little Swine opened wider. Momma leaned in and surveyed. She wrinkled her nose.

Jesus fuckin Christ.

She stood up.

Pull up your undies.

Little Swine fixed herself.

Momma went outside and Little Swine heard the sound

of running water. Moments later Momma was back with a bucket. She put it on the floor.

Here, give yourself a scrub.

Momma turned and went out the door, heaving the bolt across. Little Swine clamped her hands between her thighs, her hair falling around her face.

You prepare my goat? Momma said when Boy came back to the kitchen.

Outside, Momma.

Fuck else where you doin? Stink off you…

Nothin Momma.

Go'n take a bath, you filthy tub of shit. When was the last time you had a good clean?

Yes Momma.

Boy went out the kitchen door.

Fuckin children, Momma muttered. And then shouted: Momma's goin out for a bit.

Boy grunted.

Momma grabbed the truck keys from the counter and went out the door.

The truck pulled up outside the church twenty minutes later. The Church of Holy Providence was right on the edge of town. Behind it, and beyond, a great desert like the desert of ages, a naked expanse, a barren waste, a solitude. Here on the edge of it the house of God.

Momma killed the engine, stepped out of the truck. She squinted, looking out over the desert. Nothing moved, nothing stirred. Despite the calm emptiness of the desert Momma was not calm. Sometimes nothingness was a friend to Momma, sometimes not. She gazed over that dry relentless waste. Momma fought the anger that was her continual companion and tried to instill in herself a sense of penitence. This is where Momma came to pay for her sins.

She turned toward the door of the church. It was closed,

and had been closed for a long time. In the town of Destitution
(pop. 137) praying was a thing done behind the closed doors of
one's home, and in ways not accordant with things liturgical.
Momma prayed too, in her own way. Times she prayed for
Boy. Hurting him too was a form of praying. Way she prayed
since she was a little girl.

Momma went up the steps to the church and pushed inside.
A draft whistled through the building, subsiding when she
closed the door.

Dust on the floors, the high windows grimy and in places
cracked. The altar forlorn, bathed in a dirty light. Empty the
cold house but for a solitary figure who sat in the front pew
and stared up at the large stained-glass window. The priest,
his wide shoulders in a black shirt, his dirty hair thick and
graying. He heard Momma but didn't turn. Momma stood at
the back of the church by the door, not unsure but perhaps
waiting that God might summon her hence.

She stared at the back of the priest silently, her arms folded
across her body. Then, as if realizing someone was watching,
unfolded her arms and put them awkwardly by her side. The
priest's head tilted back a touch, as if divining the faraway
voice of a higher power. He breathed in and exhaled. From
above, the whistle of the wind through one of a thousand
holes in God's house.

Say it, child, the priest said aloud.

A pause.

Forgive me Father for I have sinned…

The priest nodded slowly. Momma fell to her knees and
proceeded to crawl up the aisle. The priest closed his eyes and
inhaled deeply. Neither man nor God knew what that nose
discerned.

When Momma reached the front, she settled, placing her
hands on her knees and lowering her head. The priest did not
turn his head, but sighed as one borne with all the world's
sins, those of man, woman and swine alike.

Confess your sins, he said softly.

Bless me Father for I am a sinner and I have sinned. I have sinned and was born in sin, and live in sin and will die therein too. Sin is all I know. Cleanse me, and free me from my burden.

Confess…

Father, only two nights ago I dreamed of the devil. He came to me in the night and breathed in my ear, and whispered a hoarse song that was the Lord's prayer but not, and a song like the Song of the Lord but spake in the blackness of his heart, and he did lie with me and sullied me with his vile words—

Enough. Don't waste my time with dreams. Confess your sins or be damned.

The priest blinked slowly and impatiently.

Father, only yesterday I did hurt a child…

The priest sniffed. Children need discipline. The Lord himself decreed it.

Yes Father.

Momma raised her hands to her face.

Tell me, he said, his fingers clawing at his palm.

I had a vile thought, Father. An incestuous thought…

Yes? His breathing quickened.

In my thoughts, I lay with a man who was my own blood, Father.

The priest's nose twitched and he bit his lip. An abomination, he whispered.

Yes Father.

A vile abomination.

Yes Father.

Little girls who have thoughts about their own fathers are doomed to rot in hell, he said. He sucked air through his teeth.

Momma stayed quiet. The priest got up and adjusted the waist of his pants. Then he turned and took a few steps toward Momma and took her by the hair. He dragged her up the steps toward the altar.

Doomed, he said again, the wrath now in him and in his

words and on his tongue.

Forgive me Father, Momma cried.

The priest dragged her to her feet and threw her over the altar. Momma looked up at the cross.

We all have our cross to bear. Momma knew it and the priest knew it, and all who prayed in their own way behind closed doors knew it. Momma, as all who like to cause hurt, was born in hurt and lived in it, and for all the naked expression of her rage and anger, needed to feel hurt too, and the only man worthy of it, the only human predestined and so qualified to cause the pain that fed her own abject and silent rage, was the father, the priest, and by that extension, God. Momma looked up at the cross and God looked down on Momma, and Momma knew that all hurt and suffering in this world was sanctioned and watched over by He above and even blessed by his very hand.

The priest lifted the weighty mass candle from the altar.

Pull down you pants, you harlot, you daughter of Satan.

Momma pushed her pants down. The priest beat her across the back of the thighs. She screamed. He beat her again. And again.

Do not withhold discipline from a child; if you strike her with a rod, she will not die. If you strike her with the rod, you will save her soul, the priest cried.

Momma screamed, the flesh of her thighs turning purple. The priest held her by the hair and continued to rain down God's wrath upon her until the candle broke. Momma's legs buckled but the good father held her over the altar.

Say ye have more wicked thoughts, harlot? the priest demanded.

Momma, sobbing, stayed silent. And then in a whisper: Every night…

The priest dropped the candle and punched her in the back. And punched her in the buttocks and the back of the thighs. And on her sex. Then he tore her underwear and forced his hand inside her.

Momma clung to the altar and called out to God and his angels. The priest picked up half the broken candle and forced it inside her until she bled.

The rod and reproof give wisdom, but a child left to herself brings shame to her father, he screamed.

He let the candle fall and Momma slid to the floor.

Her sins absolved and her vile thoughts purged, and the essential part of her fed—for Momma's vengeance upon the world was none but the vengeance of one whose entire purpose is to inflict wrongs, her herself wronged and having built her being around it—clung to the ankles of the father and kissed his feet.

Momma burst in the door of the living room where she found Boy sucking his thumb and with a hand down his pants.

Come here, you little fucking shit, she shouted.

She twisted a length of leather around his neck while Boy squealed, and dragged him down into the middle of the floor and secured him to the leg of the table that sat by the wall.

Don't you dare fucking move, she screamed. She ran out to the kitchen and came back with a wet tea towel and wrenched down Boy's pants, twisting them around his ankles and standing on them so that Boy was pinned head and foot. Boy shook. A strangled sound issued from his throat.

Don't you know what's said in the book, you impure pig?

Momma lashed him with the wet tea towel and he screamed.

Neither let us commit fornication, as some of them committed, and fell in one day three and twenty thousand, Momma said. That's in the good book, don't you hear me?

She whipped him, tortured red welts appearing up and down his back. She aimed a few shots between his buttocks, the wet towel tearing at his anus. Boy squealed.

Hear me boy? Goddamn you, hear me?

Exhausted, she dropped the tea towel and stepped away. She turned and left the room. Boy writhed on the floor, his fat back torn up.

Boy was never so slavishly dedicated to Momma as when she'd beaten and humiliated him for no good reason. After such occurrences, Boy slithered around the house quiet as a mouse, waiting, waiting, for Momma to look at him again. Boy knew better than to speak before she was ready. Instead, slug-like, he came and stood in the corner of the room, and when she left, he would appear in the next room and do the same. Eventually she would relent.

Momma made no dinner for Boy that night. Boy went to the animal shed and ate from the trough. Momma would appreciate that. That would get him back in Momma's good graces.

After eating, Boy went to the shed and looked in on Beast. Beast sat crouched in the corner, licking his armpits.

Boy went back to the house and dragged a chair to the counter and sat looking at Weasel in his cage. From Momma's bedroom came the sound of the shower. Checking over his shoulder regardless, he took a mouse from the box and dropped it in Weasel's cage. Weasel pounced on the dead mouse, catching him between his teeth around the neck. He flung him side to side and pinned the mouse to the floor of his cage. Then he dragged him inside his small shelter. Boy breathed deeply and loudly.

When he heard Momma's shower go off, he got up and went and stood in the corner of the room, facing the wall, head bowed.

He waited.

Eventually Momma came in, drying her hair. She stood still and watched him there in the corner.

Go and get changed for bed, Momma said.

Slug-happy, Boy left the room.

In the days that followed, Momma checked the calendar a lot. Boy's birthday was approaching but that was not what she awaited.

After breakfast one morning she told Boy to take Little Swine to the shower. Boy got excited. Momma twisted his ear. She didn't even need to say it.

Yes Momma, I know Momma, Boy blubbered.

Momma lit a cigarette and Boy got up.

And take her a clean nightie, she said, blowing a smoke ring into the air.

Boy took a fresh nightie and a change of underwear from the drawer and went downstairs and past Little Swine's cell. He placed her clothes on a stool next to the hose and went back and pulled back the latch and opened the door. Little Swine was sitting in her chair in the corner of the room, facing the wall. She clutched Teddy.

Little Piggie gets on the floor and comes with Boy, Boy said.

Little Swine got up and put Teddy on the chair and got down on her knees. She crawled toward Boy. Boy took her by the hair and walked her down the hall.

When he reached the hose, he pointed to the corner.

Little Piggie gets undressed, Boy said.

Little Swine stood and pulled her nightie over her head

and dropped it, crossed her arms over her pendulous breasts.

Little Piggie gets undressed, Boy said louder.

Hesitating for a second, Little Swine pushed her underwear to her ankles and stepped out of them. She covered herself, letting her hair fall about her breasts.

Boy picked up the hose and turned it on.

Piggie picks up the soap, Boy said.

Little Swine did and Boy lashed her with the freezing cold water. She let out a cry.

Piggie rubs her titties with the soap, Boy said. He stared as she soaped herself, her poor lumpy body shivering.

Piggie rubs between her legs, Boy said, and she did so. And cleans her sex good, he added.

Little Swine obeyed.

And turns around and cleans between her buttocks, Boy said, watching all the while.

Little Swine was a good little swine and did everything was asked.

When she'd cleaned and scrubbed and Boy had rinsed her off, he killed the water. He stood there watching her attempt to cover her captive body. She shrunk to the floor.

Boy put down the hose and pulled a towel from a hook, and tossed it at her. She dried herself hurriedly.

Boy pointed at the clothes.

Little Swine gets dressed, he said.

She picked up her underwear and stepped into them, tripping and falling to the floor. Boy grew irate.

Little Piggie gets dressed nice and slow like, he said.

She pulled on her underwear and picked up her nightie, and slow-like she put it on over her head and pulled it about herself, and when she was finished, good little swine that she was she got down on her knees. Boy took a fistful of her hair and walked her to the cell and inside. He led her to the bed. Without being asked, she bent over the bed and pushed her face into the mattress.

Good little piggie, Boy said. And Piggie is grateful to Boy

because he's a good boy and looks after her and makes her wash herself up nice like, he added.

Boy leaned in and sniffed Little Swine's hair.

Good piggie, he said.

He went out and closed the door and slid the bolt nice and easy into the latch. Taking care of Little Swine made Boy feel gentle like.

Boy went into the kitchen. Momma was in the kitchen. Momma was looking at the calendar. Next to the calendar was a crucifix. Momma didn't see the crucifix, but deep down in that part of herself that spoke without speaking she knew that it saw her. Momma took a pen and scratched a big 'X' through the date.

Tomorrow's the day, she said.

Boy's birthday, Boy said.

Your birthday's the day after, you dumb fuck, Momma said.

She put the pen down and opened Weasel's cage. She dropped in a cockroach and closed it up.

Momma turned and glared at Boy.

Fuck are you starin at? Sit down and eat your breakfast.

Boy sat down. Momma lifted the plate on the counter and went outside.

The shed was dark. No light shone there and never did. What lived within was a creature born in the dark and raised in the dark, and knowing only darkness it shunned the light, and made itself scarce whenever any chink of it intruded from without. Momma closed the door behind her. Within, silence. She waited for her eyes to adjust.

Where the fuck are you, you foul animal? she whispered.

From some corner, the rattle of a chain.

In there the stench of food and things rotten, and perhaps too a stench more beast than animal, for what lived within knew not the language of man nor animal and so was neither. Momma gagged. She didn't like to come here and rarely did. One bastard child was enough. The care of a beast of some unholy union was more than God could ask of her.

She stepped into the middle of the room.

You heinous fucking creature…

The chain rattles. Momma stands still. Looks around.

Silence.

Momma picked up a long harpoon from the floor and wielded it in front of her.

I dare you, she whispered. I goddamned fucking dare you.

She put down the plate. Slowly, she backed away.

Reaching the door, she dropped the harpoon and slipped out. Only when the light from outside had retreated did she hear the chain as it was dragged across the floor and the godless sound of the Beast attacking the plate.

Momma shuddered.


Momma-who-was-not-Momma was very good to Boy that night. Momma watched the shopping channel while Boy lay with his head in Momma's lap, and Momma stroked his hair and tickled his ear, and even stuck her hand in Boy's anus and made Boy melt.

Momma makes Boy all butter-like, Boy whispered, drooling into her lap.

Momma made the best butter. And Momma wanted to be sure that Boy was good and fit for the next day. Boy was not all fuckwit. He had his uses. One, at least.

Next day Momma instructed Boy to take a bath and went off into town to get the groceries. When she came back Boy was sitting in clean clothes and with his hair combed all nice. Somewhere deep in Momma's heart, something like affection stirred.

Who the fuck do you think you are? she said, glaring at him. Ain't like you're gonna marry her or nuthin.

Boy swiped his hair across his face and looked at the floor. Momma shook her head.

Go and give this to your little girlfriend, she said, opening a bottle of vitamins and handing several to Boy, and filling a glass of water.

Boy took the vitamins and the glass and went downstairs. Little Swine was lying on the bed with Teddy, sucking her thumb and gently humming. She sat up as Boy entered the room. Boy kneeled down in front of her and opened his palm.

Little Piggie puts out her tongue, Boy said.

Little Swine raised her head and opened her mouth. Boy put the pills on her tongue, pushing his finger deep in her mouth and poking around. Then he handed her the glass of water. She drank, throwing her head back. Boy took the glass from her and put it on the floor. He put his head in her lap and slid his hands up the wide expanse of her thighs.

Boy and Little Swine gonna make a baby, he whispered, groping her buttocks. Boy gets up on Little Piggie and puts his—

Boy!

A shout from above. Boy sat up. Little Swine's hands were clasped around her neck, her elbows tight together in front of her bosom. Boy stuck his thumb into her mouth, then pulled it out and stood up.

Boy was a daddy and Little Swine was a momma, and that made Momma very happy, Boy said softly.

He turned and went out, locking the door behind him.


When Boy went in the kitchen Momma was cooking. The smell was overpowering. It was a smell Boy only smelled once a year, a horrid stench, mackerel and liver and blood sausage—'breakfast of champions' Momma called it and told Boy it would put hair on his chest and make a man of him. And Boy, innocent and despicable as he was, wanted to be a man for Momma. Boy with a dog's hunger sat down at the table and waited, his eyes wide and his lips moist. The breakfast would bring out more than the man in the boy.

When it was ready, Momma put it in front of Boy and sat down in front of him and lit a cigarette. Boy went to work on the food. Momma turned away in disgust, sucking violently on her cancerstick.

Momma was on edge. A nervousness in her. A wild hope, and hope in itself does not come without an equal allotment of fear, fear that one's hopes are altogether unfounded. Momma's hope was tinged with fear, a fear that should her hopes not come to fruition then perdition was all that lay ahead.

Momma had a hope, a hope for salvation.

Boy, greasy-faced and eyes a-hunger, licked his plate clean and put it down on the table. Momma put out her cigarette.

Come over here, she said.

Boy got up and came around the table.

Take out your pee-pee, Momma told him.

Boy pushed down his pants and took it out.

Show me it's workin, Momma said.

Boy shook his pee-pee and pulled on it, and licked his hand and did it some more. Soon enough, it became engorged.

Momma-who-was-not-Momma sneered. Didn't I tell you Momma would make a man of you?

Boy grinned.

Now put it away and come with me.

Momma got up and Boy followed her out of the room and down to the basement. She slid the latch and swung open the door.

Little Swine, as if knowing the importance of the visit, was standing with her back to the wall clutching Teddy, her eyes to the floor. Boy looked at her, pulling his shirt from his pants and poking at his bellybutton.

Aren't you all nice and clean, Momma said.

Little Swine's head moved imperceptibly.

Boy stepped inside while Momma stood arms folded in the doorway.

Now you be a nice little swine, Momma said to Little Swine. Boy was already unbuttoning his pants.

Little Piggie bends over the bed, Boy said.

Little Swine with never a chance in this world. Little Swine born in chains and living as chattel, never a breath of free air to inhale or a step taken in liberty across the dry earth. Property to be used and dispensed with, and perhaps when her purpose fulfilled, to be cast away.

Little Swine did as she was told.

Little Swine exposes herself, Boy said, and Little Swine lifted her nightie and pushed down her underwear. Boy pushed his pants around his knees. Momma's anxiety grew until it was a knot in her belly and a rock in her chest and a blade in her throat, for the closer one come's to the fulfillment of one's hopes the greater the fear it will be robbed away.

Little Swine gripped Teddy tightly, pushing her face into

the bear and biting down on the dirty fur.

Boy climbed up on Little Swine, pulling at his pee-pee. He pushed himself inside her. His flexuous body sagged around her, enveloping her like a fluid broth.

Little Swine whimpered and bit down on Teddy. Momma was chewing on her knuckle.

Boy gets all up on Piggie and puts a whole litter of little babies in her, Boy uttered through his grunts. Boy puts all the little babies in her and makes Momma happy. Cause Momma wants a baby and Boy gives Momma all the babies…

Momma hated Boy at that moment with an intensity that burned her insides. Her insides seared red-hot as Boy rode and put his seed in Little Swine, grunting and sweating and to all intents nothing more than a dumb sire animal.

It was over in thirty seconds.

Boy did good? Boy said when they were done and sitting in the kitchen.

Momma sucked on her cigarette and looked at him. Boy did good, she said.

Momma give Boy the weasel? Boy said, his fists between his legs and rocking back and forth.

Your birthday's tomorrow, you little fuckstick.

Boy did good, Boy repeated, distress in his words. Momma stared at him for a long time.

Momma sucked the life from the cigarette just as it sucked the life from her, and when it was almost dead she stubbed it out, despising the cycle of life and all it bore.

She looked at Boy. Boy gets on the floor on his knees, Momma said, and Boy, trembling, crawled into the middle of the floor on his hands and knees.

Boy sticks his butt in the air like a dirty disgusting little boy, Momma said.

Boy undid his belt and pushed his pants around his knees. Momma-who-was-not-Momma looked with disdain and loathing at his fat bulbous rear.

Going to the counter, she took a pair of rubber gloves and slipped them on. She opened the cooking oil and poured it over her right hand. Kneeling down behind Boy, she stuck two then four fingers into his anus.

Boy started shaking and muttering strange incantations. Momma's whole fist and soon her arm was pushed inside Boy.

Boy moans like a filthy little fucker, Momma said.

Boy's moans were indeed filthy, and depraved and haunting and much else besides.

Momma pumped his rear as Boy moaned with pain and delight. She pushed in a second hand and spread him wide. Boy struggled. Momma kneeled on the back of Boy's calf causing him to scream with pain.

You asked for it, you dumb little fuck. Still yourself and behave.

Boy quietened down when Momma took her knee off him and he placed his face against the sticky tiles of the floor.

Momma was good to Boy on his birthday, Boy uttered. Momma gave Boy the weasel and made him cry.

Boy wanted to cry. In crying there was perhaps the purest happiness that Boy would ever know, even they be tears of anguish and pain and sorrow all.

Momma pulled her hands from Boy.

She stood up and went to the counter, lifting Weasel's cage and carrying it to the floor. She put it down and opened it. She lifted the bottle of cooking oil and lifted Weasel, and lashed the rodent with the oil and put the bottle down. Weasel struggled and clawed and nipped and bit. Momma had made sure and put the wooden block in the cage the night before so Weasel's claws would be good and sharp. Momma forced Weasel's head into Boy, and when the head was in she used both hands to slide the Mammal inside him full, and as Weasel went to work so Boy started to howl, howls unholy and demented and unheeded by any but Momma. Momma gritted her teeth and hissed and swore, and Boy, in his sad demented joy, squealed like a soul stumbled into some perverse hell.

Boy took to bed for several days and Momma brought him food and water, and like all mommas there was a kind of affection in her succor and Boy loved Momma just as she deep-down despised him.

Momma fed him and brought him salve, and Momma chopped wood and did the chores and all the things Boy was accustomed to doing, and after two days Momma was sore tired of it all and swore blind she would kill that sick demented little fucker if it wouldn't kill her in the doing of it.

She took care of Boy and she took care of the household, and she took care of that little bitch below too, and it wasn't Momma's place to be wiping the asses of two creatures that were hers but not.

One morning Momma went down quiet-like and Little Swine was licking the wall where an unpleasant blue substance was leaking through the ceiling and down the wall. Momma burst in on her and gripped her by the hair and wrenched her head back.

Fuck are you doin? Momma whispered, looking at Little Swine whose tongue and lips were dyed all blue. You tryin to poison yourself you little cunt?

Momma dragged her to the bed and threw her down on

it, then went and got some twine and tied her feet to the iron frame of the bed. She went out and came back with a wet towel and whipped the soles of her feet. Little Swine screamed and cried but Momma showed no mercy.

Count yourself lucky, you little cunt, Momma shouted. If I didn't think there was a baby in you I'd pound the living shit outta ya.

When she was done, Momma gagged Little Swine and left her tied to the bed and went out and called the plumber. A man came out and identified the source of the leak from the bathroom above and sealed it and closed it up then left.

Momma sat down. Momma was tired. Life was too much with Momma sometimes. Sometimes life was too much with her. And on those days all Momma wanted was to close her eyes and that they stay closed and never open again. Momma hoped without fear that this would come to pass.

Little Swine. Born captive and in chains all the aching-long life. Her face wet and her feet blistered and in her the sickness of those who have never been free and the sadness of those who will never know liberty. Little Swine reached about for Teddy but he lay across the floor, cast away by Momma-who-was-not-Momma whose only desire in life was to cast away all things and be free. Little Swine grappled hopelessly, tugging her legs, but the rope only cut into her swollen ankles. She swiveled her head toward the ceiling hearing only the silence. But that sound, or rather the absence of it, still rang in her ears.

The latch had not been shut.

Momma-who-was-not-Momma had been tired and angry and had forgot to lock the door behind her. Little Swine, frozen in fear for hours now, began to thaw.

She lifted her head from the bed and turned to look at the steel door, to all appearances shut like every other day as far back as she could remember, days long back into the blackness of memory.

She kicked her legs again then rolled over on her side. Her hands were free but her feet were tied, her mouth still gagged. She untied the rag that tasted of bleach from her mouth. Then she turned attention to her feet.

She sat looking at her feet for a good long while. Once her feet were untied, that was it, she could no longer pretend, and the minute Momma came down the stairs that would be the end of her. Maybe the pins or maybe the rolling pin, or maybe the towel or the grater. Once Little Swine put her feet on the floor, she was all in.

Perhaps it was some deep unfathomable intuition of the baby that had taken seed inside her, or perhaps it was years of captivity and abuse and horror, but something, the spark that is contained in all who live and breathe and know life, something was rekindled in Little Swine at that moment in a heart that had been dead for a longer time than she had heart to remember. An urge, an impulse, even a desire, arose in her and there was nought she could do to suppress it.

Little Swine untied her feet and shook her ankles loose. She crawled up onto her hands and knees then put one foot on the floor. She stood and listened. Still no sound. Only the quiet hum of the house that she had learned to discern in her stillness and fear. Putting both feet on the floor, she picked up Teddy and crept to the door. She looked around her, as if there might be part of her left behind, but she knew there was not, there was only she and Teddy and the four grimy walls that had held her prisoner for time unbeknownst.

She was familiar with the creak of the door, knew its screeches, and so she inched it open slowly and carefully, each silent groan of the hinge a deafening terror in her heart.

She slid through into the corridor, her feet pained on the damp, rough concrete. Clutching Teddy, she tiptoed to the bottom of the stairs and looked up. Through the crack of the door, she caught her first glimpse of natural light and squinted.

On tortured feet she crept up the stairs and paused at the kitchen door. Quiet within the house.

Blood thundered in her veins, her head throbbed. Her poor captive heart thumped. She stepped onto the cool tiles of the kitchen, blinded by the light from the window. Covering her eyes, she stood like that for some minutes until, slowly, she began to look about the room. She froze when she caught sight of the animal on the counter: Weasel, in a position of repose, merely stared at her from the tiny currants that were its eyes. Little Swine waited for it to screech and throw itself at the cage. It did not. Maybe it was the connivance of one who had too been captive all its short life and recognized in Little Swine's eyes the fear of the hunted and saw there its own pathetic condition. Weasel stayed silent. Little Swine crept to the back door. Having no knowledge of its whispers or laments, she pulled it slowly, the door opening with a few tiny creaks. With Teddy cradled in her arms, she stepped outside.

Terrifying it was, her first steps on God's dry earth in her poor blistered feet. Rough earth stung her soles, the weeds irritated her blisters. Above and beyond the pain she felt was both the terror of being caught and the overwhelming rush of the fresh air and the taste of open spaces. To her right, a shed. Off beyond to the left, another, from which she heard the sound of a goat. Still with the invisible noose around her neck, Little Swine moved slowly, as if tied somehow yet to her incarceration and torment. Passing the shed she heard the rattle of a chain and froze again, a terror in her heart, one that spoke an unnameable evil for which there were no words of description in any of the languages of men.

Once past the shed, the noose released her and she broke into a run, her heart pounding, her head spinning, her eyes still sore from the impossible purity of that light. Yet she saw. She saw, below her, a road, and on that road several abodes, any one of which might contain her means to freedom and safety. Beyond the road and the houses there was nothing, only a great expanse of dry earth that led to nothing and promised nothing and had nothing to give. Little Swine ran, her feet beginning to bleed. In her arms, Teddy, her sole companion and witness to her years of suffering.

She ran until she reached the road, and on the road she

kept on running until she reached the first house. She banged on the door to no avail, and she banged some more and kept on banging, realizing eventually that there was no one within to aid her. Little Swine got on the road and kept running.

Under the evil heat of the afternoon sun, sweat poured from her, and with her bloody feet and the drenched nightie on her back, and the tortured and defeated look about her, she was as bedraggled a being that had ever been seen on those highways. Reaching the second door she banged on it too, and a woman appeared there, a shotgun in her hand.

Little Swine croaked a cry for help, forming no words that might convey her sorry plight. The woman stroked the barrel of the shotgun.

I think you best be gettin outta here, said the woman.

Little Swine held up Teddy, as if Teddy might elicit the sympathy she could not.

Ain't no fuckin business of mine, whatever you're into, the woman said. Now like I said, you best be leavin.

Little Swine made a last desperate plea for aid.

The woman's eyes sparkled with hatred and malice, and fear also, as if things stirred behind her own doors, dark secrets buried there too that the arrival of this poor tortured spirit threatened to release.

Get the fuck off my porch, the woman said, raising the shotgun and pointing it between Little Swine's eyes.

Tears and sweat and desperation marked her face, but faced with no other option Little Swine backed away, stepping down into the road. She turned and ran.


Heaven knows what it was stirred Momma. Certainly it was no noise, for there were none loud enough to wake her. Boy lay silently in his room, the trauma of days before still on him and keeping him subdued in the bed. Perhaps it was the sudden absence, a privation, even loss, that caused her to open her eyes and look about the room confused like and feeling an unfathomable tug at her heart.

She sat up and lifted the glass of water and sipped, then opened the cigarettes, took one and put it in her mouth and raised the lighter to the end. But before she could light the thing, she froze, listening intently, some aberrant rumor of the house upsetting her. She took the cigarette from her mouth and put it on the bedside table along with the lighter and stood up and went into the kitchen. Seeing the door open, she knew. She looked at Weasel as if his eyes might betray what he'd no doubt bore witness to. Her eyes bored holes into the animal, then she turned and hurried down the stairs.

She stood at the open door of the cell and stared inside, the absence now renting something within her and causing her knees to buckle. Momma screamed, a wail that contained therein the suffering of several lifetimes and the hell that gave birth to them, and therein too the loss of all redemption and hope of redemption and the eternal damnation of a lost soul.

Momma fled up the stairs, snatching up the keys for the truck and fleeing out the back door. She hopped in the cab and tore down the drive in a fury, and into the road almost crashing into the yucca at the bottom of the drive.

It was about halfway to the church she saw Little Swine. Her fat little body rumbling as she ran half-naked to some faraway, never-to-be-reached salvation. Hearing the truck, Little Swine turned and saw Momma in the distance, and immediately turned off-road and began to race into the expanse of the desert. Still clutching Teddy.

Reaching where the little bitch had run off-road, Momma turned the wheel and raced after her.

You little fucking cunt, Momma screamed, you ain't taking my fucking baby away from me, do you hear me? You fucking little cunt…

Momma drove right over the top of Little Swine, the truck jumping as the wheels tore over her lumpy body. The truck screeched to a halt. Momma got out and took her by the hair.

You little fucking bitch, after all I've done for you, this is how you repay me…

She dragged Little Swine by the hair and threw her into the bed of the truck, and tied her by the neck to the bars of the back window of the cab. Broken and bloodied as she was, Little Swine still clutched Teddy to her bosom.

Filled with fury and retribution, Momma jumped into the cab and ripped home.

Boy was standing in the kitchen door when Momma returned. He watched silently as she dragged Little Swine down the stairs and into the cell and dropped her on the floor. She came back up the stairs, face still lit with fury and righteousness.

What you're gonna do, you fuckwad, since you're in good health again, you're gonna go and take that fucking beast out there and let him in the room with that little cunt for an hour. Go. Now.

Boy's face turned white.

Fuck are you waitin for?

Momma no, Boy uttered.

Fuck you say? Go and do like I fuckin told you…

No Momma… Boy's baby. Momma's baby…

Fuck the fucking baby, Momma said.

She stuck two pointed fingernails up Boy's nose and pulled him to the back door.

You go and do like I fucking told you, or I swear, I'll hurt you like you've never been hurt.

She pushed Boy out the back door. He turned, once, to look at her. Seeing the look on her face and understanding the intent of her, he stumbled to the shed and inside. Momma watched.

She licked her lips, her mouth dry, impossibly dry. She turned and went into the bedroom and locked the door behind her. Her hands shaking, she picked up the discarded cigarette and lit it, and sucked it half down before letting off and exhaling.

She never heard Boy come in the house. She never heard him go down the stairs. But ten minutes later she heard the screams from below, screams which she heard and Boy heard and would never again unhear, but which no God nor angel heard nor any being besides, for the screams of Little Swine were such that all horror was contained therein, and it is the tragedy of all God's creatures who dwell in misery that on some days God has no truck with horror.

II

A baby was born and brought into this world without hope or happiness and lived beyond the first dry screams of its issuance into this life of pain and suffering. Little Swine did not once hold her baby in her arms; it was ripped from her by Momma and taken away, and she was left on her bed of torment in the blood and afterbirth which fell from her in bringing a child into this hateful world. Catatonic as she was, it was no hardship to her. Momma continued to drip-feed her and force-feed her, and once a day she would come and milk Little Swine so the baby might grow in the sustenance of the one who bore her, but Momma-who-was-not-Momma had no doubt who was the child's rightful mother. It was what Momma had been waiting for all her life, for in motherhood she saw redemption and a way to break the evil of past affliction, and in raising a child and nourishing and teaching her, she would earn redemption for her sins and the sins of the father. Momma would come to live in Christ, and Christ would come to live in her too and know her and love her and forgive all. Momma saw the way now.

Boy, too—even if he could not fathom good and evil and the way and the light—was changed.

Boy's a good daddy, he would say to Momma when he sat down next to her in the evening as she cradled the child. Boy hold baby?

Not tonight, Momma said, and said it every night.

Boy's a good daddy and Momma's a good momma, he said.

Momma said nothin.

Perhaps Little Swine dreamed in her black catatonia. Perhaps deep within that dark place she retreated to there was something, buried fathoms down in her core, that still cradled the seed of the life she might have had if things had been destined to go a different way. Perhaps.

But nights or days when Boy came down and lay next to her on the bed and whispered softly in her ear any childish inanity that came into his head and even sang her sweet lullabies, no intimation of those buried dreams was seen in her cold dead eyes and no lullabies sung deep in her heart, and even when Boy climbed up on her and enfolded her in his lumpen corpus and put himself inside her and rocked back and forth for half a minute, no seam or vein of emotion was uncovered, not joy nor hatred nor loathing nor even disgust. To all the world, which for her was Boy and Momma and the four walls of her cell, Little Swine was dead inside.

And for Momma that was just fine, for all that Momma needed of Little Swine was for her to keep producing milk, and when it came time that the child could be weaned off the mother's milk and onto something else, then Momma could get rid of Little Swine and be free at least of one part of her burden. Momma had it all planned out, and despite the world of hurt that lay behind and despite the cold echoes of certainty that her history bespoke, Momma was sure her plan would come to fruition.

And Baby—what of its dreams?

Who knows of what babies dream. Of substance we know naught, but one can be sure the dreams of babes are filled with soft turquoise-blue waters and tender expanses of green, and rainbows and reveries and the softness of breasts and fountains of milk everlasting. Perhaps too they dream of the abundant tones of earth's undulations that exist as the music of unheard worlds, privy to the ears of babes and the more primitive animals but not to those who have grown and been perverted by the earth's corruption. All these things babes might dream of, and yet, beyond the walls within which she was born existed no such blues or greens or gentle music, only endless burned expanses that suckled nothing and fed nothing, and indeed did the opposite, which is to say bled the animate and all things living, and in that denial was the essential truth of all their lives: That dreams are dreams and life is suffering, and while the two may co-exist, in that world of unholy nothingness, both were deadly and constrained by the terminal inevitability of tragedy.

Little Swine lay on the bed and sucked her thumb. No turquoise dreams for her. No gentle music or soft green expanses. No hope. But even deep in her catatonia she did register the cries of Baby, her flesh and blood and issuance of her womb, and she registered too the cessation of those cries and Baby's provision, for Momma in her twisted way did see to Baby's needs. And if Little Swine had in her own way died, then some part of her did live on in Baby, and the ebb and flow of Baby's needs in this world was the only needle that recorded the basal state of Little Swine's consciousness.

Little Swine lived but for the intervention of Boy and Momma.

She heard not their coming down the stairs nor the latch in the door, nor reacted when Boy placed the tray on the bed and sat with his back against the wall, and took her in his arms and rested her head against his shoulder. He tilted her head back and lifted a spoonful of soup and brought it to her mouth.

Piggie is a good little swine and eats for Momma so Baby can grow up big and strong and make Momma and Boy happy, Boy said.

He pushed the spoon between her lips, tipping the soup onto her tongue. Then he tilted her head back yet further, letting the soup slide down her throat. She gagged.

Good little piggie, Boy said.

He did it again, patiently too, spoon by spoon until much of it was down her throat, but as much too had dribbled down her chin and onto her chest and between her breasts. Boy put the spoon down and mopped it up with his fingers and pushed it into her mouth.

Dirty little piggie, Boy said, as he slid his hand into her nightie and groped her breasts with his soup-sodden fingers, and squeezed and pinched her nipples.

Piggie has to eat so she can make milk so Baby will stop crying and be happy and Momma won't shout, Boy said.

He laid Little Swine down on the bed and put the tray on the floor, then he lay down beside her and took a breast from her nightie, putting it between his lips and sucking on it like a swollen, overgrown baby.

Piggie's milk is good, Boy said, and he squeezed her breast and sucked on it hard.

Boy?

The shout from upstairs.

Fuck you doin?

Boy pushed her breast back into her nightie and put his face into her hair and licked her cheek. Then he got up.

Comin Momma, he shouted.

Boy brings Little Piggie somethin special next time he comes, Boy said, all excited like.

He went out with the tray and put it on the floor and locked the bolt and went upstairs to Momma.

That little swine eat? Momma said.

Yes Momma, said Boy.

Good. Go fetch me the breast pump, Momma said.

When Momma had milked Little Swine she hooked her up to the drip. Basement curative. Little Swine curled up in the fetal position and sucked her thumb.

Above, the baby began to cry. Momma thought Little Swine

twitched, and stood and looked at her for some time.

Think she's your baby? Momma said with a sneer.

No answer.

She ain't your fuckin baby. She's my baby, and don't you go thinkin any different.

Momma glared at her.

The fuck do you care anyway? You're nothin but a fuckin vegetable.

Momma picked up the milk. I'm gon' feed my baby, you hear?

She went out the door and slammed it, sliding the bolt into the latch.

Fat, useless fuckin piggie, Momma uttered.

Boy hold baby? said Boy.

Fuck off, and stop fuckin askin, Momma said. Go and bring in some wood for the stove.

Boy got up and went outside, and Momma rocked Baby in her arms, her child sated and satisfied and asleep, unaware that he slumbered in the arms of Momma-who-was-not-Momma, but what did Baby care? So long as he had food and warmth, Baby was just fine. Who knows, maybe deep down she was aware that the one who held her was not her flesh, and not her blood, and was not the fount from which she had sprung, but if she did, she was none the bitterer for it. Baby slumbered while Momma-who-was-not-Momma watched, Momma's cold and suffering heart perhaps feeling for the first time in her long tortured life that just maybe she could feel something that was not terror and not hatred or vitriol, but something… something else. Momma smiled a smile that was no smile but rather a long-suffering grimace, but nonetheless felt like a smile. From the kitchen she heard Boy deliver wood to the old metal bin next to the stove. One more burden that needed to be discarded, and why not? Once the little bitch downstairs was dispensed with why not take care of the idiot fuckwit too? That would only leave one burden in her life, the oldest and fiercest, but if she was to be free after all, then loose ends would need to be tied. And when they were, it would just be Momma and Baby, and together alone they would take the life that Momma never had, and she would give Baby any other life than what hers had been. They would live together and flourish and grow, and make each other whole.

Boy put the wood in the bucket, Boy said.

Good, said Momma. Now go and feed Beast.


Weeks or months into his short life, Baby cried a lot. Momma didn't know how long the little soul had been on this earth; nights were long and Baby needed care, and Baby was keeping her up nights and Momma wasn't sleeping. Days, nights, went by, and Momma grew more and more agitated. She found herself on the verge of snapping at Baby or worse, but to her credit she held back and did no harm to the poor little soul.

But something crept into Momma, some evil suspicion, a haunting guilt, a terrible accusation with which she began to flagellate herself morning, noon and night, until it became so great Momma went to the bathroom one day and took a razor and ran a bath. She got into the cold water with the razor and sat there with the steel to her arms, pressed to her flesh so that blood dripped into the water. But could she do it? Momma gritted her teeth and pushed the razor into her taut skin but could not muster the strength to drag it along her arms and release the demons that so tormented her. Tears came to her eyes, and Momma rarely got so that tears came to her eyes. She put the towel in her mouth and screamed, and slashed her legs up and down the thighs, outside her right thigh and on the inside of the left, and on her abdomen too and even her right breast. The bath filled with blood and Momma continued to scream and weep, but she could not bring about the end she'd so desired for more years than she could remember.

From beyond the bathroom door, Baby began to cry.

The demons spoke to Momma.

The demons spoke to her in her waking hours and in the depth of night, and even spoke to her too as she rocked and fed Baby. Momma feared for Baby. Momma feared for Baby so much she decided there was only one thing she could do: Momma had to murder the demons, and to do that she had to murder him that had birthed them and set them upon her and bade them their doing yet.

Momma had to murder Father, for by murdering Father she might bring to an end the sins of the father and release Baby from the cruelty of generational sin. Thus was her salvation and Baby's salvation assured, and only by murder might she ensure the child knew life.

Momma fed Baby and put her in the cradle. She put the cradle on the kitchen table.

She went to Boy's room and put him on the floor and tied him by the neck to the frame of the bed and left him there.

Momma gon' be back real soon, she said, and she went out. Putting a pacifier in Baby's mouth, she stroked his cheek and went outside.

In the animal shed she took the boning knife still tainted with the blood of the baby goat and slipped it inside her bra, below her shirt right beneath her armpit. She went out to the truck and climbed in the cab.

The church was forlorn in the late afternoon sun. Its walls cracked, paint faded, the steeple askance and the bell long silent, this was no house of God but a testament to his absence on this earth.

Momma killed the engine and got out of the truck.

The fear was in Momma.

A lifelong fear, now accumulated at this very juncture, where Momma was forced to face the devil and put a knife in his heart so he might release his grip on Momma and she might be free of his demon host. Momma's hand went to the blade of the boning knife. Nestled there beneath her vest, it was her and Baby's only salvation.

Momma wanted to vomit. Her mouth dry and her heart tight as if someone clenched it in their fist, she held onto the bonnet of the truck, her legs buckling under her. Out beyond the church, the great nothingness, the unholy absence, the spring of all that is barren and hostile and anathema to the living. Momma looked out and knew that should she fail in her task, that was what awaited her: the great nothing, for if she could not free herself to save Baby, that was all she deserved.

Momma looked up to the roof of the church, atop of which sat a great vulture. She blinked her eyes and saw a vision: her body lying prone in the vast nothingness, her bones to be picked dry and returned to the bed of all things.

Momma wiped the sweat from her brow and went up the steps of the church and opened the door.


In his room, Boy needed to toilet bad. Momma was mad at him and he didn't know why she was mad, but Momma only locked him up when he'd done something bad. Boy clawed at the rope around his neck but Momma had him tied up good. Boy wasn't getting out. But Boy was gonna pee himself if he couldn't get free.

Boy decided it was better to pee on the floor than pee on himself, so he opened his pants and took out his pee-pee and peed over the wooden floor between his legs. One of Boy's greatest pleasures was peeing. Boy smiled and shook himself off and tucked his pee-pee away.

Outside beyond the door Boy heard Baby cry.

Baby is cryin but Momma isn't around, so Baby stops cryin, Boy said.

But Baby, having no heed for Boy nor anything else in this world but his own base needs, did not stop crying. Baby was hungry, or maybe Baby had soiled himself. Baby was upset.

Boy grew agitated. Boy fought with the rope around his neck, choking himself. He kicked at the air, and when he almost passed out, he ceased struggling.

Baby… Boy saved Baby, he shouted, his voice a gurgle in his choked throat.

Clinging to the rope, he kicked and gave up.


In the dark fog of her consciousness, Little Swine's hand slipped inside her nightie and took a hold of her breast and pulled it out. She pushed her nipple into Teddy's mouth and squeezed, sending a trickle of milk into Teddy's mouth.

Shhh, she whispered, the sound raspy and broken, no noise other than whimpers or screams having issued from her throat for a long time. She stroked Teddy's head as she fed him, above only the rattle of the bed to which Boy was tied and his guttural panicked shrieks. Little Swine tended to her little ward and gave no mind to the cries above. Tiny was Little Swine's world, the circumference of her cares not extending beyond that of her tired and broken body.

Shhh, she whispered, her milk trickling over Teddy's head and down onto the stained mattress.


Momma stopped inside the cold vault of the church. From outside she heard the terrible rasping screech of the vulture.

He was there, the priest, the father eternal, sitting in his place in the front pew, a place he would sit until Judgment Day should Momma not deliver judgment upon his head before that day was out. Momma stood still watching the evil slope of his shoulders, his head held high, to what heavens he appealed Momma could not and never would guess. Her hand went inside her shirt where she fingered the bone handle of the knife. She gripped it tightly, her eyes closed, then let go.

She took a few tentative steps down the aisle.

At the sound of her footsteps, the priest's head cocked, upward and to the side. Her footsteps did not cease.

The priest spoke, his voice a stone command in the cold parliament of the church:

Child, honor thy father and mother as the Lord thy God

commanded you, that your days may be long and that it may go well with you in the land the Lord your God has given you.

Slowly, deliberately, Momma walked on up the aisle.

The priest stood, standing in the aisle to look at Momma as she drew close.

The priest sucked air in through his teeth. Momma stopped only feet from him. They looked at each other for a Godly second.

If a man has a stubborn and rebellious child who will not obey the voice of his father, the priest boomed, and though he discipline her she will not listen to him, then the father shall take her out to the elders of the city and he shall say to the elders of his city, *This my child is stubborn and rebellious; she will not obey my voice.* Then all the men of the city shall stone her to death with stones. So you shall purge the evil from your midst, and all Israel shall hear, and fear.

If Momma was afraid—and she was—she showed it not. Her two hands were clasped in front of her that they might not tremble and give her away.

I have a child now, she said.

Some strange contortion betrayed the face of the priest. Momma saw and took a step toward him. Now she had to twist the thorn.

I have a child of my own, my own little girl, she said. She's yet a babe, tiny, beautiful, innocent…

At the sound of that word a twitching attacked the face of Momma's tormentor.

Innocent and pure as an angel, she is. And you know what? She's gonna stay that way. Because you will never, I repeat *never*, see your—

Before Momma could finish the sentence, and before she could react, the priest lashed out with the hand, catching Momma on the face. Fury overcame him. His face was painted with all hell's venom as he, with the agility of some demonic imp, pounced upon Momma as she fell with a cry.

He took her by the hair and dragged her toward the altar, throwing her to the ground in front of it.

Momma's senses came back to her, and her hand went to her armpit. But the priest had her pinned by the hair to the floor. He began to scream.

A child? A child! I gave you a child… I gave you many children, you whore cunt, don't you remember?

He struggled with Momma's belt and ripped down her pants.

Many children I gave you in the grace of God and you and your devil mother killed them all. Do you remember?

Momma's hand found its way into her shirt and gripped the handle of the knife.

Remember?

The priest fumbled with his belt as he held Momma pinned to the floor. He extracted his member and climbed up on Momma.

A child is it? You want a child? I'll give you a fucking child…

He forced himself into her.

Momma gripped the knife. All she had to do was pull it out. She could get him in the leg. In the side. Maybe even the eye if she got it right. But her hand stayed as the priest committed his vile rape upon her.

For the Lord disciplines the one he loves, and chastises every child he receives. It is for discipline you have to endure. God is treating you as his child. For what child is there whom his father does not discipline? the priest screamed in her ear.

The priest dripped his poison into Momma, the lash of his spit on her face. Her teeth gritted, her eyes stinging, fury in her, yet her hand was like stone on the handle of the knife. It moved not.

Panting, he spilled his demon seed in Momma as he bit her face. Then he collapsed on her.

He lay there heaving, Momma frozen under his weight, her hand still clasping the knife.

When he got up and crawled off her and climbed into the pew, he closed up his pants and fixed his hair, and stared up at the broken stained-glass window above. The archangels still flew, the cherubim still on the wing, the whole host of God and his angels resplendent in their heavenly glory.

Outside the vulture cried.

Momma didn't move. She lay there gripping the knife's handle, her face wet and her hair about her face. Even now, even now she might. Even now she might save herself.

But there was to be no salvation. Instead, Momma got up onto her hands and knees and crawled down the steps to the aisle, and crawled up the aisle on all fours, her pants trailing after her. The priest did not look, but he delivered some parting wisdom to Momma as she went:

For the moment all discipline seems painful rather than pleasant, but later it yields the peaceful fruit of righteousness to those who have been trained by it...

Reaching the door, Momma crawled out into the white heat of the afternoon and to damnation.

Boy slipped his neck from the tether and got up onto his knees and took hold of the bed frame. He stood up and looked about the room as if in confusion. The sound of the baby crying caused him to turn his head. He followed the sound to the kitchen where he found Baby in his cradle on the kitchen table. He looked down at the babe, who looked back up at him and let off crying for a bit, before starting again. Boy picked up the child. He held the baby at arm's length and began to shake him gently.

Baby was good for Momma, he said. Baby was good for Momma and Momma didn't get sad or mad no more.

Baby wasn't sad, or tired. Baby was hungry. Boy held Baby in his arms and rocked it. Baby did not stop crying. Boy grew anxious.

Baby stopped crying and was good for Momma, he said again.

Baby did not stop.

Boy put Baby back in the cradle and put the pacifier in its mouth. Baby stopped. Boy turned his head to the staircase.

Little Swine was still feeding Teddy when Boy opened the door. Seeing her heavy, voluminous breast, Boy stood in the door and stared, his tongue sliding from his mouth to lick the corner of his lips. Then he stepped inside.

Kneeling next to the bed, Boy inhaled the heady smell of warm milk and looked at the trickle of white that dribbled from her nipple. He took Teddy from her hand and lifted her tit to his mouth and began to drink. She did not respond. Holding her tit in two hands like a large coconut, he sucked the warm sustenance of her manna. Little Swine's milk was plentiful.

When he'd drunk his fill, he got up on the bed and lay next to her, pulling her arm around him. He pushed her hand into his pants.

Little Piggie is a good momma, Boy said.

Little Swine stirred.

Momma is good to Boy, she whispered.

Boy froze, stilled by a voice from one who had hitherto been voiceless.

Momma is a good momma to Boy, she said softly.

Momma? Boy whispered.

Momma is good to Boy and takes care of him, Little Swine said, her broken untrained voice with a kind of unearthly succor.

Little Swine squeezed Boy's pee-pee and pulled gently.

Momma…

What does Momma do for Boy? Little Swine whispered in her voice broken and holy.

Momma gives Boy the fist, Boy said, squirming in delight.

Momma gives Boy the fist, she repeated.

Boy turned around to look at her with his slug eyes, before getting up and climbing onto all fours. She sat up. She looked at the twine that was still tied to the bed frame. Taking it, she tied Boy's feet, and Boy, in his sluggish innocence, did not object.

Momma gives Boy the fist, Boy said.

Momma gives Boy the fist, Little Swine said.

Then she picked up Teddy. She smiled at Teddy, a tiny, wry smile on a face that still bore all the horrors of the world and much besides. Then she twisted off Teddy's head.

Turning it inside out, she revealed a diabolical contrivance: a glove of sorts, on it hundreds of pins, all plucked from Boy's fleshy corpus over many years, forgotten remnants of Momma-who-was-not-Momma's flippant tortures. The pins were embedded into the plastic base of the lamp and sewn into the head of Teddy. Little Swine slipped it over her hand like a glove.

Momma gives Boy the fist, Boy said insistently.

Momma gives Boy the fist, she said.

Then she punched him with all her strength in his testicles.

Boy screamed and tried to pull away but his legs were tied. Little Swine leapt on his back, preventing escape. She punched him again, and again, in his testicles and in his penis until they were nothing but bloody strips of flesh both, and when she was done, she went to work on his anus.

When her work was finished, she stepped down off the bed and looked at Boy who lay there in a river of his own blood, squealing like a trapped pig. She watched and waited as he bled out, cradling little decapitated Teddy in her arms.

Momma came through the back door of the house, bruised and tattered and with the stink of damnation on her. Baby was crying again. Momma's face, streaked and defeated, twisted in agony. She approached the table and looked down at the child. The babe writhed and contorted, and squealed and cried, and Momma cried too, for she saw that there was no salvation for her nor the child nor any issuance of hers that would come after. Momma screamed, and in that scream all the hopelessness of living. Then she picked up Baby and flung her at the wall.

Baby's little body broke and cracked and fell to the floor. Baby squealed no more.

Momma, whether for herself or for Baby, cried tears of sorrow. Momma's time had come; there was no way back and no way forward, and no hope of forgiveness. She went to the cupboard, atop of which sat the shotgun. She reached up and took it, and fell into a seat at the table. Lifting the shotgun, she put it in her mouth. She closed her eyes. Her face wet with a river of tears, one might even have thought there was hope for her soul.

Momma bit down on the barrel and gripped the trigger.

Momma?

The voice was one unknown to her or any other, one which

had lain dormant for a God's age and which now found articulation there in that demented house at the center of the desert of God's earth.

Momma opened her eyes. Momma saw an angel, a beatific angel bathed in white and with God's holy aura around her and carrying what appeared to be a holy cherub.

Momma?

The angel walked toward Momma. Momma looked up at her in rapture.

Child? she whispered.

The girl stabbed Momma first in one eye and then in the other. Blinded, Momma fell to the floor screaming. In her sudden darkness, Momma crawled toward the door.

The girl picked up the shotgun. She shot out one of Momma's legs at the knee, then the other. Limbless, Momma-who-was-not-Momma writhed on the floor in blood and anguish.

But the girl was not done. Taking the shotgun she went out to the shed where the Beast dwelled. There in the darkness where evil lurked she stepped quietly across the floor. But evil did not scare this child no more, for angel or not, she had taken judgment upon herself and no man, woman or beast was to be exempt from its charge.

In the middle of the floor, the girl kicked an empty food tray. The beast sprung from the darkness.

The girl put a hole in it. She watched as the thing thrashed on the ground, the sounds from it nothing natural to the ears of men. She put two more holes in it for her own recompense taking care not to kill it, and when she was satisfied the thing would die slowly and agonizingly, she went out.

Momma on the floor still, drowning in her own blood.

The girl put down the shotgun and picked up the poor broken babe and put it in the cradle and took it outside. In the shade of a cedar, the girl dug a hole and buried the child, cradle and all. She said no prayer over it and no God watched over her, and no angel or host was there to sanctify the burial.

When the fruit of her loins was in the ground, the girl took Teddy and left that place and did not look back.

On tired and broken feet the girl walked across the field and across the brush, around her a wide and vast expanse filled with nothing and promising nothing, but for all that an open and unencompassed world which for her, on feet which had hitherto known only cold concrete and the confines of a tiny cell, was a thing of great and almighty wonder. The girl cradled the teddy bear in her arms as she went, in no hurry and in no particular direction, the red welt of the evening sun approaching the horizon with something like errant malaise. The girl saw no malice in it, nor did she fear the onset of night. She was a being much akin to darkness and much befriended to it, and, resolved to her free passage over this, the wide and unencumbered earth, continued unabated. This time her bare uncovered feet did not register the prick of the hard soil or its dried and rebarbative weeds, instead every stab of the callous ground was a reminder of all that was left behind and would never again be so. Indeed, with every step away from the house the girl felt lighter, freer, as if she might indeed be an angel come across a land that God had long since abandoned.

Before long the girl reached the road and set out on the road toward the setting sun. She looked ahead, unperturbed by the long listless highway that lay beyond. And indeed, in the red of the setting sun, the look on her face of grim resolution soon softened, and even something akin to a redemptive smile came over her visage.

She walked, and it wasn't long before she passed the church, to her a broken and tumbled shrine to God-knows-what, alien and disarranged in that red and brutal landscape, perhaps more akin to a mausoleum than a place of worship. The girl paid it no heed and walked on, Teddy still nestled in the crook of her arm.

Soon a truck approached her along the road ahead, pulling up as she neared and stopping beside her. The girl stopped and the window rolled down. In the cab of the truck, a priest. He looked her up and down, seemingly unperturbed at her ragged and unearthly appearance.

Where you headed child? he said.

The girl didn't reply.

Heavens above, you look like you need a good dinner and a bath. Why don't you jump in and I'll take you up to the church and get you something to eat?

The girl looked down the vast endless highway at the red sunset, and back at the priest. Compelled by some unearthly law or unspoken demand of the heavens, she climbed into the cab of the truck.

The priest looked at her.

Good Lord, but your momma must have abandoned you, he said.

The girl said nothing.

And who's your little friend?

Teddy, the girl said.

Well, what say we go and all get better acquainted, you and me and your little friend here? the priest said.

The girl turned to look out the window at the vast desert of the earth, knowing in her heart that she had no fear of anything that lay beyond herself, not God nor man nor any beast or angel in between, not even the devil nor his host nor any being spawned therefrom. And knowing it, she was thus ordained to be the executioner of a will that was in her and beyond her and contained of a power that obeyed not only the law of the earth which is that of life and the living, but the taking and the cessation of it too.

The girl looked down at Teddy, stroked his head and smiled.

END

## The Cottage

*Men are men until they encounter evil. And after, they are compelled to do evil itself.*

Turning their backs on New York, John and Katie Mears purchase their dream home in colonial Connecticut, the place they hope to raise their firstborn and build life as a family. But the cradle of the American nation has a haunting past, and they find themselves swallowed by a dark history, one of blood and anguish, a specter of the country's painful birth in the slaughter of pilgrim times. The dark crucible of the nation is yet manifest. Blood debt is eternal, and sooner or later history calls for retribution. It is the blood of innocents that pays for the sins of the father.

## The Sistema Series

There is a company that provides a deeply sinister service for shady clients: subconscious torture for political or corporate manipulation. Vangelis Zervas is an agent of Vathos and does his job with zero qualms. But when a young boy is killed over a highly coveted piece of software that may have been produced by the company, the boy's mother goes in search of her son's killers. Meeting a group of disparate rebels with their own hostility toward Vathos, they join forces to bring the company down. Vangelis Zervas is on their radar, but will he see his way to help them and go rogue, or stay true to the devil inside? Sistema is a dystopian/cyberpunk horror that journeys into hell itself in exploration of man's search for power and control.

## Meat

In the murky wake of the financial crisis a string of establishments pop up across Europe catering to a hedonistic underground, its clientele beholden to a strange, hallucinatory meat. Stoked by the fleshy and charismatic Hugo and fuelled by voracious consumption of ecstasy, the craze spreads from the heart of Europe all the way to the Mediterranean, where in Athens the financial elite begin to turn on each other. Murder, barbecue and apocalyptic raving ensues, culminating in the most savage party Mykonos has ever seen. Follow the story to its destructive end, where consumption eats itself alive.

## Notes from a Cannibalist

1847. Assuming the identity of a dead Jesuit priest, a survivor of the famine in Ireland travels to South America where he is tasked with rebuilding the missions among the natives. Inducted into local life, Father James Carmichael finds love with a native woman and becomes acquainted with the ways of the Guaraní, discovering ayahuasca and ritualism. In a battle with his own gods and demons, the priest fights for the life he envisions, his own self the ultimate stake of the struggle. Worlds are shattered, realities crumbled, lives destroyed. His soul victim to the crucible of the New World, what is tempered in the chaos will be outside his control.

## A Whore's Song

Hidden away in the backstreets of Amsterdam is a secretive whorehouse, open only to those in the know, where torture, pain and extreme sexual sport are the vehicle to understanding and self-knowledge. Run by the obscure Madame Zhu, the establishment is a magnet to the city's elite and mad soul-seekers alike. Two lives collide in a chaotic downward spiral brought about by psychoactives and sexual torture when, over the course of a day, a whore recounts her life as a destroyer of egos and one man is forced to face his deepest demons. Cast out into the far reaches of his mind, will he make it back from the other side?

In a world where the weak become prey and strength means brutality, living may come at the cost of dying first.

## The Book of God

*God isn't dead. He's just a bit mental...*

Indignant at his corrupt and ignominious creation, God sits and stews in his treehouse outside the small town of Brawl. His only companion and sole remaining attendant, a withered and tortured scribe, chronicles the Lord's descent into madness as he struggles to collect all the lost souls which have escaped his records and further addled the Lord's already woolly mind. But when the Scribe is forced to hire a maid to care for the Almighty, the introduction of a buxom woman into God's life brings chaos in its wake. And what's more, the maid has an innocent and attractive young daughter...

Suffering rejection, humiliation and loathing of humankind, God seeks a way to bring back Christ and trigger the Apocalypse. The only thing standing in his way? God's old harpy of a mother...


## The Jaguar

1849. Salome Azul, daughter of a powerful politician, flees Buenos Aires at the height of the Argentinian civil war. In London she enlists the help of Irishman Sean Ryan to open The Nightingale, a high-class brothel and opium den that will be used to entrap and blackmail London's political elite.

In doing so she will make enemies. What's more, Ms. Azul has carried her own demons from Argentina, and it is these that will prove her most relentless foe. In order to survive, she must eliminate all weakness from her character. Doing so may mean cutting away all she cherishes most.

In the pursuit of power, unrelenting sacrifice is what decides who lives and dies.





## Pietro Aretino's Dialogues

Nanna has been a nun. She's been a wife. She has also been a courtesan. And now, as her daughter turns sixteen, she must decide how to advise on her path in life. On what route should she send young Pippa?

Bawdy, filthy, hilarious and uproarious, listen to Nanna regale her friend Antonia with scandalous tales—tales of seduction, blasphemy, lies, dishonesty, thievery, nastiness, cruelty and treachery—in an attempt to decide on what course to set her daughter: should she be a nun, a wife or a courtesan?

Ultan Banan started writing as a way of getting his head straight, discovering in the process that staying busy is the only way to stop oneself going insane. He devotes what time he can to writing, doing his best to avoid gainful employment by increasingly creative means. He lives on the move but dreams of a small cottage on a foul and inhospitable coast somewhere. Currently  in Scotland.

Latest news at
ultanbanan.com

Substack:
ultanbanan.substack.com

Twitter:
twitter.com/ultanbanan